NOW OPEN SUNDAYS!

NOW OPEN SUNDAYS!

A Celebration of Faith from a Church with a Message

REV. PAUL SINCLAIR

PORTICO

About the Author

When Paul Sinclair was recently asked if he is still a practising church minister he replied, 'Yes, I'm still practising, but I've not mastered it yet!'

Rev. Paul Sinclair was born and bred in Glasgow. It was during his apprenticeship as a sheet iron worker on the shipyards of the River Clyde he became a Christian, was baptised and joined the Church of God, an Evangelical Church, where he learned the importance of the Gospel. From there he moved to the Elim Pentecostal Church, studied at the Elim Bible College and was assigned to Kensington Temple, the biggest Pentecostal Church on the British mainland at the time. He was then seconded to the Willesden Revival Centre with his colleague Gareth Lewis to re-launch the work there. Due to popular demand Gareth returned to Kensington Temple and Paul stayed on to complete the adventure recorded within these pages.

Although he was ordained by the Elim Pentecostal Church in 1992, just three years after starting in both Willesden and Kensington Temple, Paul is convinced that being a Minister of the Gospel isn't determined by carrying the title Reverend, but by demonstrating an 'adventurous walk with God'. As a 'Minister of the Gospel' Paul has preached at churches, schools and motorcycle rallies in Scandinavia, Ireland, the United States of America, Romania, Peru, Nigeria and South Africa. He has written for the motorcycle press, various newspapers and the Christian press as well as finding himself featured in numerous books. Paul is regularly interviewed on national radio and television and, most recently, appeared on Robbie Coltrane's *B-Road Britain* and the BBC's *Two Feet in The Grave* with Richard Wilson.

Above: Paul, right, with Father Scott Anderson on the day they blessed the Ace Cafe, London

Paul's tenure in Willesden ended after a road traffic accident. While recovering he launched the first ever motorcycle hearse service in the UK, the original (and famous!) Motorcycle Funerals Limited (www.motorcyclefunerals.com) and secured the Sidecar Hearse patent. Today his company runs its own manufacturing unit where the hearses are built and strategically based professional hearse riders serve in various areas to cover the entire UK with by far the largest fleet of motorcycle hearses in the world.

Paul is married to Marian, from Ghana, West Africa, who is a trained counsellor and enjoys singing as a ministry. When time permits they ride a 955cc Triumph Speed Triple and although Paul does not own a car he does borrow Marian's sports car from time to time.

Despite being a truly non-conformist minister of the Gospel, Paul is not against organised religion because he believes it is safer than disorganised religion when looking after children and youths, but ultimately he believes in a simple walk with God. That is what Adam had and then lost, so when he meets folk who have lost it, he just wants to see them get it back.

HOLY SMOKE!

We've signed a sponsorship deal made in heaven, by backing Willesden's Reverend Paul Sinclair, the famous motorcycling minister. Dubbed the 'faster pastor', we had no hesitation in supporting Paul's much publicised fundraising work for his church youth group. With College House just down the road, our own motorcycle guru Ian Smith said: "It really is a case of love thy neighbour!"

Wagon's Ian Smith (right) shows his thanks for a divine sponsorship deal with the Reverend Paul Sinclair (left)

TOMB RIDER

Rev's sidecar hearse

This book is dedicated to all the people who, over the years, told us these signs made them laugh, made them smile and made a difference to them on their way. To all those people who helped me make them and encouraged me to carry on hanging them up, thank you.

Foreword

Paul Sinclair – you might not always agree with him but you certainly cannot ignore him.

I first met Paul when I was conducting an Evangelistic Mission in Paisley, Scotland. He was about 19 years old. I recall challenging the young people of the area to dedicate their lives to God's service, many came forward for prayer and Paul was one of them. As I prayed for them individually all of them fell onto the floor overcome by the power and presence of God, but Paul was the only one that did not fall, which goes to show it is not all in the manifestation. Look at what God has done with him and through him.

This excellent and exciting book reflects Paul's character and personality as it presents God and the Gospel in a humorous yet powerful way. Just as you cannot ignore Paul, you couldn't ignore his eye-catching signs and posters outside his church in Willesden. No wonder the newspapers and TV stations got involved with Paul and his church. Ignore him? Never.

I was a regular preacher in Paul's church and witnessed many manifestations of the presence of the power of God in transforming lives, healing of the sick and bringing peace to the troubled soul. As I read through Paul's draft of the book it kept me laughing and enjoying the precious truth of the Gospel. It's a must-read for both Christians and all others, and is a great Evangelist's tool.

Rev. George Miller, International Evangelist

Left: The Willesden church as it was in the early 1960s

Introduction

My great-great-grandfather Charles Baxter spent a full five years going up the Amazon in the mid-nineteenth century. This was just a few years before David Livingstone reached the Victoria Falls. How dull life would be if people didn't have a go at reaching out? Reaching out is both an adventure and a reward. Churches are not inanimate objects, they are groups of people that believe in God and they need to reach out too.

To understand the significance of this book you need to grasp the unique strategic position of our church in the British mainland of the 1990s. Harlesden and Willesden were statistically ranked the two worst areas for violent crime in the UK and our church occupied the border where the Harlesden and Willesden statistics were drawn up. Amazingly, and not without irony, we opened our doors to preach the Gospel of Peace with God in the most violent place on the British map at that time.

We saw our Wayside Pulpit – using signs to entice people in to the church – as a way of reaching out. We wanted our community to know we were here and to connect with them in their daily lives. I don't take credit for the idea of the Wayside Pulpit as it dates back years and most likely to pre-Columbus times. My 'Signs and Wonders' mentor was the Rev. Brian Grist who was infamous for his often controversial posters in Carlisle. I decided to take a different path and make my posters even bigger and to be as topical and relevant as possible. These signs would be the bait with which I'd fish!

'Come, follow me,' Jesus said, 'and I will make you fishers of men.'
Mark 1:16-20

As well as reaching out our colourful posters provided the community with something to laugh about and even boast of. Willesden wasn't a 'crime statistic' or a 'downtrodden place,' it was an area alive with people who were a joy to serve and as we pasted up the signs many would stop to chat, so many sometimes it took hours to hang a single poster! Such was the friendliness of our community.

Many of the signs that are not in this book are missing, sadly, because the photos were either lost or never taken at all. One in particular, 'The wages of sin are still the same, even with inflation,' went down well, but sadly no picture of this remains. 'Now Open Sundays!' was a real sign and once served as the church's telephone directory advert as well. One Nigerian minister, Reverend Peter Obadan, who became a key part of our William Hill story (on page 57), came as a direct result of the signs – he was determined to be part of an outward-looking and reaching-out church while here and that's exactly what we were.

Our Wayside Pulpit at Willesden was very successful and it constantly made the national and international press as well as the international television, radio and internet too. More importantly it connected with our local community and helped people in many ways, but *even* better than that, it caught fish.

It would be absurd to suggest that every church should follow suit with our signs, but it is only right to hope that all readers be inspired, encouraged and refreshed in their understanding of God. God is not dull and he too is reaching out to you, so without apology you will find me present the Gospel to the unbeliever and simply encourage a walk with God.

My great-great-grandfather made a remote place he'd never seen his goal. For the reader who has never seen God, I challenge you to make Him your goal.

Rev. Paul Sinclair

In *Now Open Sundays!* I have an inspirational, and original, adventure to share. Our story tells of a fight to save a church from being torn down and how the Queen, Defender of the Faith, helped us. I will also tell the story of how we sought to buy a successful William Hill bookmakers next door to our church and will also share numerous enjoyable incidents that happened along the way. But right at the outset, on this very first page, it is important to give credit to those who made our story possible at all ... my predecessors.

Give everyone what you owe him:
If you owe taxes, pay taxes; if revenue, then revenue;
if respect, then respect; if honour, then honour.
Romans 13:7

In 1960 Frank and Phyllis Preudhomme were asked to commence a Pentecostal Church in Willesden. One day, Mrs Preudhomme noticed an old stone step protruding out from under some huge hoardings. She got on her knees to discover an old church door. The council explained this was a derelict building that had previously been a billiards hall and it was soon to be pulled down.

With a council representative, Mr and Mrs Preudhomme crawled under the hoardings to get in. Because of the darkness they needed a torch, the floor was full of water as the roof had completely disintegrated, the windows were smashed and there was no toilet, gas or electricity. But this did not matter at all. An immediate leasing deal was struck and, along with the new congregation, the Preudhommes set to work on building a church! Mr Preudhomme worked so hard he rendered himself a double hernia and no one took a salary to pay for it all, such was their passion.

As the building was transformed the congregation took meals to the elderly and, as a former English teacher, Phyllis taught the literary programme for those coming to the area from the West Indies. At that time, prior to the current housing rules, the council would also phone if they needed help finding homeless people accommodation. The church always provided. As well as this vital social role the church became a well-known evangelistic centre.

After Pastor Frank Preudomme died, Pastor Phyllis carried on faithfully right up until 1988.

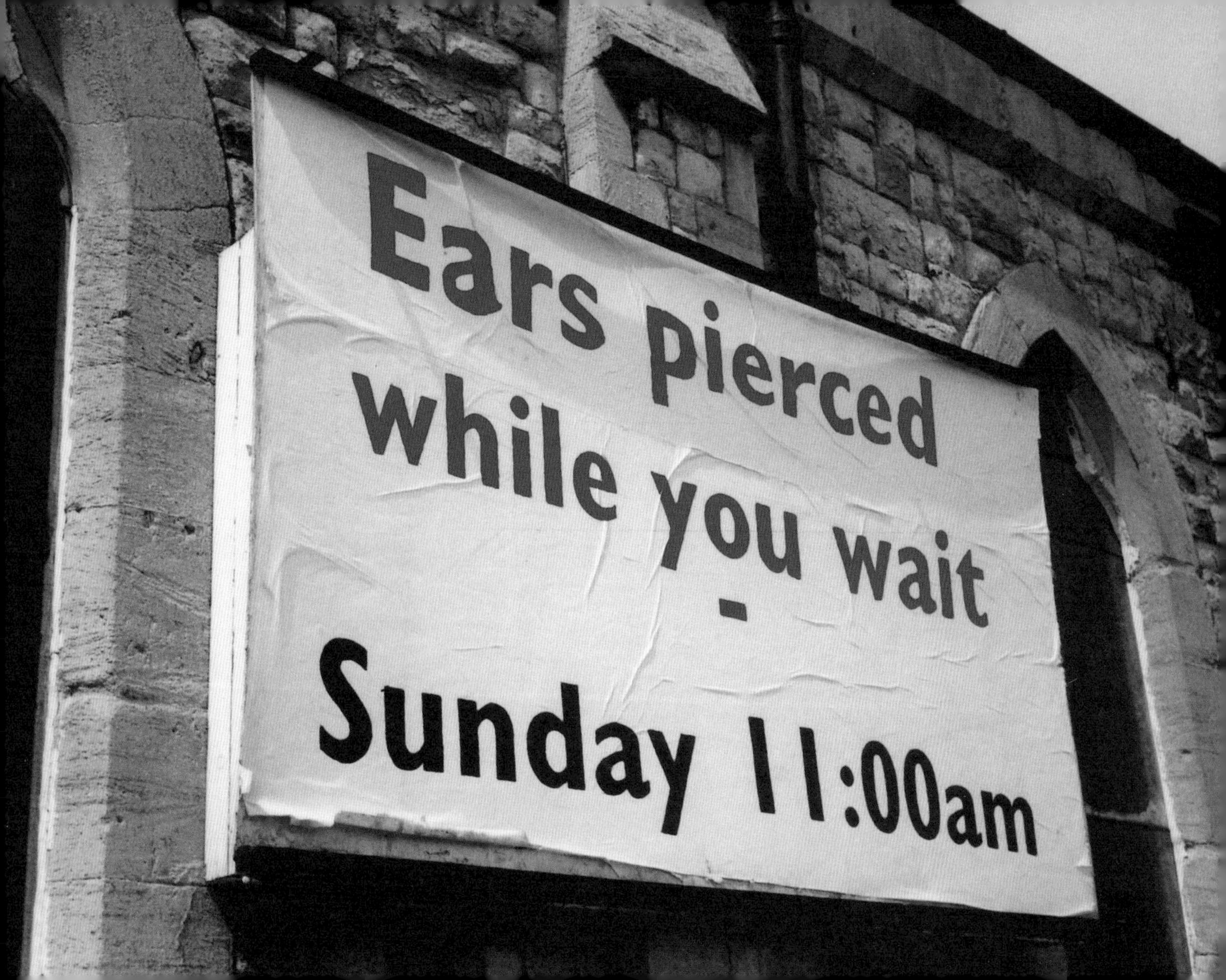
Ears pierced
while you wait
-
Sunday 11:00am

I was keen to promote a healing service at the first opportunity I could once I had become a minister, but on the day of the first service the healing evangelist called in sick! A few months later I tried again with another one and he couldn't make it because his wife was ill!

I am the Lord, Who heals you.
Exodus 15:26

Gareth Lewis, my colleague at the church, was still in Willesden with me at that time so together we finally hosted a crusade –

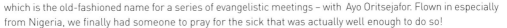

which is the old-fashioned name for a series of evangelistic meetings – with Ayo Oritsejafor. Flown in especially from Nigeria, we finally had someone to pray for the sick that was actually well enough to do so!

This is a humorous story, of course, but numerous people who suffer are used to alleviate the suffering of others. In my home church, the Glasgow Elim Pentecostal Church, God used our old Pastor Kelly to lay hands on a lady who suffered the very same terminal predicament that his own wife was dying of. Sometimes the Lord heals people straight away while others are left until later. When Jesus healed the man at the pool he walked past many to get to him and then away from others when he left; he has a timing all of his own and that would not have been popular. Some are healed so much later they are actually with him when he finally does it.

It is understandable that someone in a position of suffering should resent God because of illness, but God uses people who suffer to alleviate the suffering of others. For those who are in discomfort this is a remarkable way of turning a difficult situation on its head.

Serving on the pastoral staff of Kensington Temple as our new congregation found its feet had its challenges. Years before my granny had told me I had a face that only a mother could love and then pointed out that even my own mum would go out without me! My mother was no better – the name Paul is derived from the Latin word 'small', so when I asked why I was named Paul she told me that after taking one look at me 'we never thought you'd come to anything.' Glaswegians can be so cruel! It is said that being good-looking is a curse and if that is the case there was no way my grandma thought I was cursed! To rub salt in the wound there were other, single, trainees assigned to Kensington Temple and one was a very smooth, sophisticated young man called Chris Denne.

And these signs will follow those who believe:
In My name they will cast out demons;
they will speak with new tongues;
they will take up serpents;
and if they drink anything deadly,
it will by no means hurt them;
they will lay hands on the sick,
and they will recover.
Mark 16:17-18

At Kensington Temple we believed God for miracles and many people testified to what God had done and still do. In our tradition, during a service, we simply invite people forward for prayer and then the pastoral team will stand at the front and lay hands on people to be healed. It didn't take long to notice Chris Denne's prayer line was always longer than mine! Mostly with ladies, and ladies of all ages, I might add. Chris would still have a queue even as the rest of us set off for coffee after the service. As with me, he was sent to a smaller church, but his congregation grew much quicker than mine. He seemed oblivious as to why his predominantly female congregation grew so much faster than any other. Later, they moved him somewhere else and this happened again and, it seemed, everywhere he went to preach a good turnout was always guaranteed!

nowing, cold and bleak. Around this time, my flatmate Charles' Egyptian girlfriend Theresa was due to drive up to Scotland to visit one of her friends, so he decided to come and join me for a few days with my Scottish uncle and aunt in Dumbarton.

The Scots were nice, welcoming people, and always good for a laugh. Paul took me to Hogmanay that New Year. It was quite an experience. The highlight of the trip was when I had to ride behind Paul on his motorbike so he could take me back to meet Theresa for the drive back to London. It was dark, cold and foggy, and I was riding with the Faster Pastor, as Paul is known, trying to beat a time deadline. It was scary, to say the least. Several times on the journey I committed my life to the Lord and thought about my family in Ghana and how I was never going to see them again!

Don't ask me how, but Paul got us there. I've lived to tell the tale. They say hindsight is 20/20. Ask me to do it again today and I'd rather walk the sixty or so miles we had to travel that night!

Charles Hammond

No one knows when their last journey will be so why put off walking with God now? Next time you are headed on a journey and you see a church, stop. Just as your vehicle needs a service, so do you. Think about it, it could be your last service for a few miles!

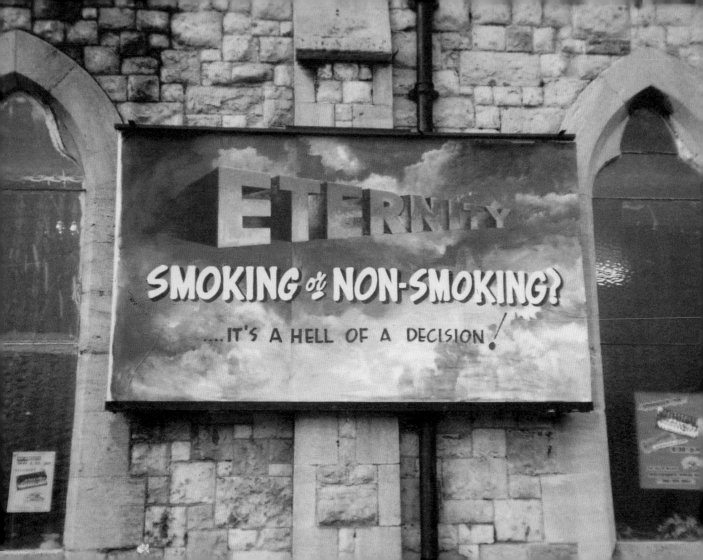

One Sunday my mentor at Kensington Temple, Rev. Wynne Lewis, announced, 'Tonight at 6.00pm Dr William Atkinson will be addressing the very serious subject of Hell, to which I give you all a very warm welcome!' On another occasion he told us Rev Ian Paisley – a veteran politican and church minister in Northern Ireland – had been preaching on Hell and in his infamous booming voice proclaimed, 'there will be wailing and gnashing of teeth.' According to my old boss someone put their hand up to point out they had no teeth, to which the Rev Paisley replied, 'Teeth will be provided.'

For this is the way God loved the world: He gave his one and only Son, so that everyone who believes in him will not perish but have eternal life. The one who believes in the Son has eternal life. The one who rejects the Son will not see life, but God's wrath remains on him.
John 3: 25-36

Pentecostal ministers, such as myself, are often portrayed as fire-and-brimstone preachers who would scare the Hell out of you, while Anglo-Catholic Priests are seen as woolly liberals, but in my experience nothing could be further from the truth. During my tenure in Willesden Father Scott Anderson, a thoroughbred rocker and clergy biker of the Church of England, arrived at the local parish. Contrary to stereotype Father Scott preaches on Hell once every year as a discipline. Meanwhile a sad number of Pentecostals, perhaps because of the fire-and-brimstone stereotype, feel pressurised to present a politically correct and easy-to-swallow picture of a 'nice' God. Some folk take this to an extreme and present a whole new cuddly and fluffy, wet and insipid God who has nothing better to do than run after us with his arms open wide. Even the cartoon God of *The Simpsons* is tougher than that!

The fear of the Lord is the beginning of wisdom.
Proverbs 1:7

Our small Willesden congregation struggled to afford a salary during the first few years so I worked as a motorcycle courier during the day and a youth worker some nights to make ends meet. The Green Party were making headway at the time, and proving to be quite popular, so 'Green' issues were topical and once, riding my dispatch motorbike on London's Old Street, I drew alongside a van with a great caption on the side, 'None of our jokes are tested on live animals.' I couldn't resist the adaptation for a church sign! Getting music played at our church was sometimes a real struggle. I played my guitar and a professional musician called Jonathan Wales created backing tapes to help us at no charge at all. Musically we struggled but over time we developed a fantastic team and even launched a touring group, The Counsellors.

Make a joyful noise unto the Lord, all the earth: make a loud noise, and rejoice, and sing praise. Sing unto the Lord with the harp; with the harp, and the voice of a psalm. Withtrumpets and sound of cornet make a joyful noise before the Lord, the King.
Psalms 98:4-6

The media portray church services as dreary, boring and dead (possibly because they often are!), but a church can only be as good as the musicians that go there to perform. I noticed that our Wayside Pulpit helped attract seriously good musicians and it is my hope that any musicians reading this book will go out and hunt down a musically-struggling church and transform it until it's kicking!

young ministers are subject to reviews from older and retired clergy. One Sunday a retired Rev. Jack H. Davies appeared to assess my performance. After the service he told me my preaching was 'a masterpiece of miscommunication'.

It pleased God by the foolishness of preaching to save them that believe.
1 Corinthians 1:21

With the great bible teacher, and disciplinarian, Rev. Colin W. Dye as my immediate ministerial example and the challenge of reaching his high standards, my preaching skills eventually improved. A few years later, I was invited to preach in Nigeria where most preachers are reknowned for being pretty lively, so I thought I'd be more dramatic and decided to go for it African-style! Dramatically, in a town called Ife, I threw my hand in the air with abandon. Unfortunately, I hadn't noticed the huge metal air fan directly above me and my thumb got whacked so hard it jammed the fan! I had to be taken to hospital after the service.

A later invitation to preach led me to the Christian Center, Fort Worth, USA, where Steve Vanzant and his pastoral team work tirelessly to serve the underprivileged. As an illustration of sin I began to cut up my tie – I'd been doing this for years and it was a fool-proof illustration that I learnt from Rev. Brian Grist. At first sin is minor, so you cut off the tip of your tie, but you hide that sin by tucking it under your belt, then cut off another bit as the sin gets bigger and hide it under your jacket and so the sermon goes on. All was going well, except that I was wearing a tie mike and the cable was attached to the back of my tie. As I reached my crescendo there was an almighty bang, the sound cut out and my sermon reached an abrupt end. That day I discovered what 'rolling in the aisles' meant. These Texan folk were howling and even crying with laughter as Pastor Vanzant gently led me away!

A dmittedly this caption on the right is as old as the hills; in fact I wouldn't be surprised if it was Adam himself that made it up! Young ministers tend to think they can change the world overnight, but after a time reality hits home. Some blame others while some blame themselves, but the smart ones stop to take stock. In our church it dawned on me most people had been Christians longer than I'd been alive and those in their thirties had been attending bible studies since I was a child. This meant the entire congregation knew the bible better than me. So why was I there?

> **Don't let anyone look down on you because you are young,**
> **but set an example for the believers in speech,**
> **in life, in love, in faith and in purity.**
> **1 Timothy 4:12**

I concluded it was my job to help them reach out so one day I nervously preached a sermon called 'Scratching where it itches'. Playing a track from the Sex Pistols I made the point that youths are attracted to anything that scratches where they itch and we too must address the issues they are thinking about such as their careers, relationships and sex. As I looked over the stone-faced congregation there was no doubt in my mind both the Sex Pistols and this message had just signed my fate. It was time to pack my bags before I was thrown out! Mrs Cox, a West Indian lady and a real character, grabbed my arm and grinned. 'Ohhh,' she said, 'I'd love a young man like you to teach me all you know about sex!' As I turned violently red Mrs Amory, another stalwart of the church, asked for a word. 'This is it,' I thought, 'I'm finished now'. Instead, Mrs Amory told me she had been considering leaving the church but, after my sermon, and believing in its message, decided she would stay. True to their word, the residents of Willesden and Harlesden all reached out together and the church steadily began to grow.

Mrs Amory and Mrs Cox stood by me through thick and thin, they had taken in a boy and stayed the course until he was a man. When they were satisfied they had done their job they went to be with the Lord. Their philosophy of life was simple: rather than blame me when I got things wrong they would build me. They were one up on Adam and Eve!

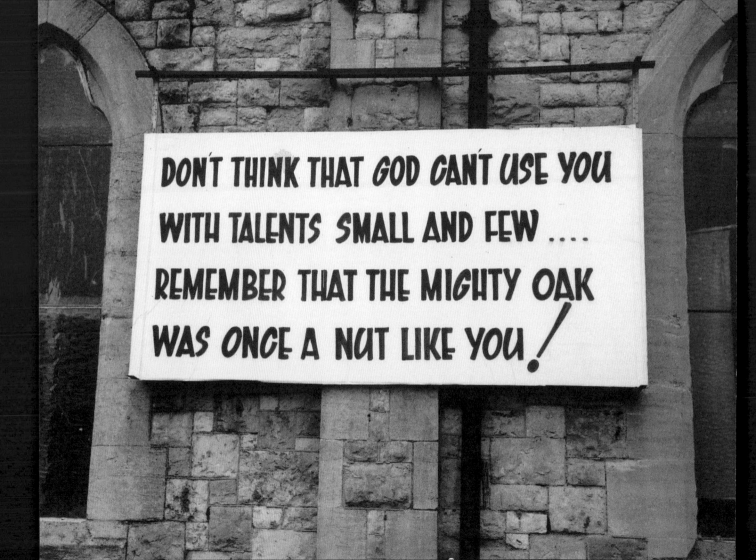

he only way to develop a reaching-out church is to let the members develop and find themselves. Raquel Sims is now a member of The Plops, a popular band in New Zealand.

This is her Willesden story:

Someday, somehow, I wanted to be a singer, but at all the young adult camps, meetings and talent quests I was there singing out of time, sometimes out of tune but always with 200 per cent.

While attending Willesden church I decided to go for it and became a student at London's School of Creative Ministries. My assessments required I give a sermon and have my Pastor sign it off. I spent hours preparing, I was nervous. I mean, after all, I had the famous Paul Sinclair, 'speaker of all speakers', ticking the box. Regardless of my nerves I spent quite some time praying and sincerely searching God for the words to say. The emotion was high, the dramatics were on fire and when I came to close we could have heard a pin drop.

'Lord,' I said, 'I know you gave me the words but far out! I rocked just then!' Quietly I closed my bible. Still numb from the nerves I told myself to keep calm, keep looking like I know what I am doing and no one will ever know. Secretly full of myself I looked out on the sea of touched faces, praised God, smiled and humbly left the plat...form...

The video shows my disappearing off screen to the banging crash of me tangled in a mess of microphone cables ... *who* left the microphone cord on the floor??!

Oh well, thanks Willesden church, 16 years later I'm a professional singer.

Raquel Sims

his is the only poster we ever ran twice because the bible is often seen my many as some useless old book. As with the telephone directory the bible can be pretty dull to read, but not when you are looking at it with a reason, a purpose. The phone book comes alive when you need a plumber or realise today is your wedding anniversary and the same is true with God's word, the bible.

Your word is a lamp to my feet and a light for my path.
Psalm 119:105

We ran the poster 'Know Jesus – Know Life, No Jesus – No Life' to promote the visit of Norman Robertson, a gripping bible teacher. At one of the meetings the Holy Spirit guided him to ask if the person who wanted to have children but hadn't would identify herself. My friend Eileen Christie put her hand up. Although bible verses should not be turned into incantations to try and get God to do things for us like some sort of machine, the Holy Spirit does lead us through his Word and what we see should be taken seriously. Norman Robertson and Eileen marked passages about healing and confession of faith so that she and her husband, also a church minister, could speak them out and hold onto them. Today they have two children.

The bible provides answers to where you will spend eternity, find help in times of need, a way forward when all else fails and also to success. So dust it and trust it.

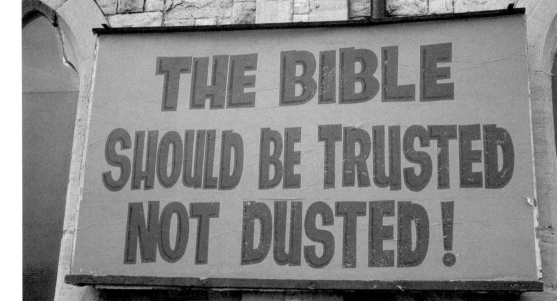

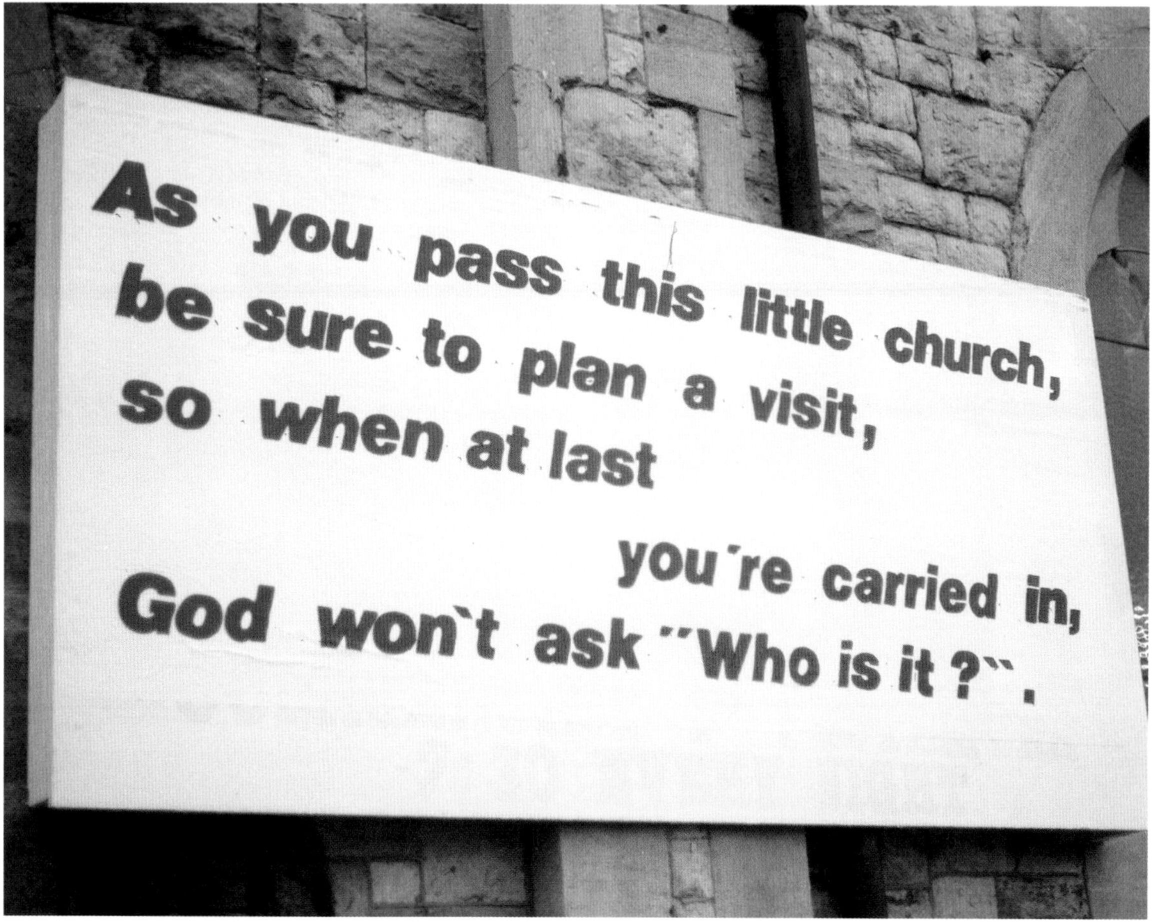
As you pass this little church,
be sure to plan a visit,
so when at last
you're carried in,
God won't ask "Who is it?".

Our Wayside Pulpit was directly opposite the rear gate of Willesden Bus Garage. One night a man was seeing his brother off and together they had a good laugh at this particular poem we had put up. About two years later the man knocked on my door to tell me this story because that was the last time he ever saw his brother again. He had died. This man wanted us to know how much it meant to him to have the last memory of him and his brother laughing at our sign together.

Having a major bus garage directly opposite the church had its downside. On a couple of occasions our wall had to be rebuilt due to buses rolling back when the handbrakes were left off and during one service there was a colossal bang. We all ran out to find the small car of one of our most faithful ladies, Samantha Thomas, had just become a micro car! We couldn't believe it. On one occasion we had a visit from an American preacher. He had been so exhausted from his travels that he'd fallen asleep on the bus only to be woken up in the bus garage. Cheapest fare for a guest preacher we ever had!

Boast not yourself of tomorrow; for you know not what a day may bring forth.
Proverbs 27:1

Many see no point in being buried or cremated by a church minister they have never met. With reference to the funeral service they have a good point, but they entirely miss the point as regards death. Although the body ceases to function life does not, it is not suddenly all over. One way or another each of us will meet God, so best to do it now.

For many years the media presented racism as a white-on-black problem. As the BNP made gains during this time this intensified and white folk in predominantly black or Asian areas – like Willesden – were left with no voice. Racial attacks and victimisation on white people were left largely unchecked by the press as they targeted the BNP. This left white clergy in predominantly black congregations in a predicament, especially when even some church publications began to push for black leaders, 'the future of black churches!' – I personally suffered my cheekbone being cracked and other injuries in a vicious racial attack, but when I called my uncle in Dumbarton he said he 'was ashamed of me.' "But there were loads of them," I protested. "Aye," he replied, 'but they were English!'

Our congregation was made up of black people from Great Britain, the West Indies and Africa, but it really bothered them when anyone called them 'a black church' because they dearly desired our church to be more representative of our area. We were one on this so I preached a sermon entitled 'I'm dreaming of a white Christmas' and we decided to get the message out we were a church for Allsorts.

At this time the 'Black is also available in White' advertising campaign for John Player cigarettes was running and seemed popular. Huge hoardings would show a number of black fish with one white fish, some black London Hackney cabs with one white cab and so forth, each with the caption, 'Black is also available in White'. This would be an expensive poster to produce as it had to perfectly match a professional advertising campaign in order to work, but it was my opportunity to address a highly charged and tense topic with a grin. For the sign, Kensington Temple Gospel Choir lent me their best-looking black singers and I did what any native Scotsman would do, I clapped out of time.

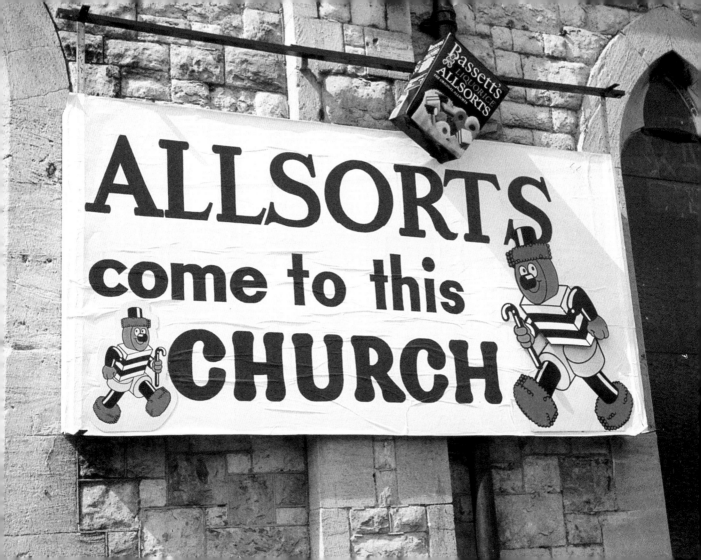

Ray and Mary Pryce-Williams were the first white couple who came through our doors. Ray was a Rhodesian-born professional sign-writer and until the day he died he painted all our Wayside Pulpit signs. Mary being Irish was an added bonus as most of the white people in our area were Irish too. On request, Trebor Bassett kindly sent us a Bertie Bassett model to hang outside and Ray got to work with the Allsorts message. Now we were gunning for Asian folks as well as whites.

All did not go to plan as someone stole the Bertie Bassett model. Rather than despair I decided to invest in a stamp and sent a letter to the local paper about my concern that Bertie may have been kidnapped. This made the front page of both the paid and free papers so the whole community got the message we were not a one-colour church any more, but a church allsorts went to!

Iron sharpeneth iron;
so a man sharpeneth the countenance of his friend.
Proverbs 27:17

Over the years our congregation suffered frictions as cultures inevitably clashed and jealousy between groups would rear its ugly head, but at my final service nine years after the two racial combatant signs went up I stood in awe at the congregation. There were Malaysians, Asians, South Americans, Latin Americans, whites, blacks and Orientals. There was no predominant group at all and even the whites were a mixed bag of British, Eastern Europeans, Irish and so on. The video tapes of our last month's services prove we really did incorporate every colour in the Willesden area.

en Livingstone is my political hero. I don't agree with everything he says or does, how could I, but as my local MP and a man who would later return to his old haunt opposite the Houses of Parliament after eighteen years with the words, 'before I was so rudely interrupted,' you have to love him.

In 1992 Red Ken, or Pink Ken as the Communists called him, was running for another term in Brent East. To my delight he based his campaign headquarters opposite our church complete with a large billboard the same size as ours. Despite his political genius Red Ken had become Red Rag to a bull. As quickly as possible we copied the colours, font and layout to launch our own campaign and even invited the candidates for a Brent East version of *Question Time*.

As a younger man I had clear political views, but no clue about politics! In my naivety one candidate duped me into not inviting the Communist Party to *Question Time*. When I eventually realised I had made a mistake I carried on with the plan rather than admit my fault. With the Conservative pro-life candidate Damian Green standing and the debate being held in our Pentecostal church the Communists were convinced there was an agenda.

Question Time went well until a planned point where we were vigorously interrupted by Communist activists in the most noisy and colourful fashion imaginable. I can however report that various colours of spray string were fired at us and not just red. This time I faced up to my gaffe and I invited their candidate onto the stage. Their leader was an impressive young lady called Mrs A Murphy and when she heard me at least acknowledge a mistake and invite her up she took her place with great dignity. My one regret was not making a proper and formal public apology, so (deep breath) here goes: I'm sorry Mrs Murphy...

Jesus Christ
Campaign Headquarters
Question Time: Tuesday 31st - 7:30pm
with all constituency candidates for Brent East

Picture of *Question Time* line-up (left to right):
Mrs A Murphy – Communist Party, Ms Theresa Dean – Green Party, Mark Cummins – Liberal Democrat, Damian Green – Conservative, Ken Livingstone – Labour, then me.

The Gospel is not anti-Communist, anti-Capitalist or anti-Green. Neither is it anti-Socialist, anti-Liberal or anti-Nationalist and I don't mind letting the cat out of the bag when I say it is most certainly not anti-Scottish Nationalist! As a minister of the Gospel, I'm not somehow better than any political candidate who is sincere in their attempts to improve the world, but it is my duty, my job, to preach the Gospel. Politics can bring change, but only the Gospel can bring change that is everlasting. No politician, however adept, can resolve your long-term standing with God.

I sinned against a candidate and her whole party. Fortunately for me this particular candidate was as gracious as she was smart so she forgave me and moved on, but that does not resolve my ultimate gaffe, which was with God. This is where Christ comes in, thanks to his death on the cross and resurrection we can ask him for forgiveness.

All the believers were together and had everything in common.
Selling their possessions and goods,
they gave to anyone as he had need.
Acts 2:44-45

Ken Livingstone was duly elected MP for Brent East once again and, at a time when so many are disillusioned by so many politicians, I must tell one more story of Red Ken. Tony Kenton of the Rotarians invited me to give a talk one day at one of their early-morning breakfast meetings. Tony is a model Rotarian dedicated to helping community projects. As it was autumn the leaves were falling, the mornings were crisp and being invited to such a prestigious group I felt like a knight in shining armour as I arrived on my beloved Honda Fireblade motorbike. As I roared into the car park I could see Tony ready to welcome me. What I didn't see, because of the leaves, was all the mud. A man of great distinction and seemliness, Tony was polite enough to wave as both I and my bike gently slid past him!

Having arrived with a bang the meeting went well and I told the story of Ken Livingstone and his Campaign Headquarters sign. 'If you could get him to speak here we'd give your church £500,' one of the members quipped. Not one to back away from a challenge, I immediately typed a letter to tell Ken of this man's rash offer. I heard nothing back until some weeks later we received a Rotarian cheque for £500 – Ken had gone as speaker to help us out!

I can't support all Ken Livingstone says and does, but any public servant who really does care about their community deserves to be noted.

ur congregation was becoming a mix of colours and ages and as you will see later, there came a point where we had twice as many men as women, but at this infant stage the church was still predominantly female and we needed to get the message across we were also male-relevant. Clint Eastwood is a man's man and no one would consider him weak. Jesus was also a man's man and yet for years he has been portrayed as a wimp in a negligee carrying a sheep. Why would a carpenter carry a sheep? It makes no sense! As well as being strong to do his work Jesus would have tough hands and, because of where he was born, dark skin. Despite all this he is portrayed in books as a white and blue-eyed effeminate wimp. We wanted to communicate the fact that Christianity is also about men's men, but in my typical good humour.

This Clint-inspired sign promoted the fact that we too welcomed the good, the bad and the ugly and sure enough it wasn't long before lots of ugly people started coming along! The Clint Eastwood posters proved very popular and the final of the three signs we planned said 'Sunday service 11.00am - Remember to bring a fistful of dollars!'

Aware of the fact Clint Eastwood played golf in Scotland I sent copies of the sign to him and invited him to the church. Clint has a good reputation in Scotland and when volunteers at a Scottish Christian drug and alcohol rehabilitation unit wrote to celebrities asking for signed photos to auction off, Clint Eastwood was one of the first to send one. Unfortunately though, a reply (see overleaf) came not from him, but his solicitor, and politely asked me to take it down.

July 21, 1993

Rev. Paul Sinclair
Church On The High Road
Elim Church
334 High Road
Willesden, London
NW10 2EN, England

Dear Rev. Sinclair:

    We represent Clint Eastwood.

    We are informed that your Church makes use of photo-graphs and other likenesses of Clint Eastwood as well as slogans with which Mr. Eastwood is identified.

    While we appreciate your motives and good intentions in this respect, such uses of Mr. Eastwood's likeness, persona and identifying symbols create a problem for Mr. Eastwood which we are confident you did not consider. Generally speaking, uses of Mr. Eastwood's photograph, likeness, posters and slogans with which he is identified have been limited to utilization in and in connection with motion pictures. Since Mr. Eastwood, naturally, has the right to control the use of his name, likeness, persona, etc., we have accordingly been successful in restricting such utilizations.

    Thus, we would be grateful if you would be good enough to permanently remove the signs and posters which make use of Mr. Eastwood's photograph or likeness, including slogans identified with him.

    We trust you understand the nature and purpose of this request and that you will accommodate us in this regard.

    Please accept our thanks for your cooperation.

    Sincerely,

cc: Clint Eastwood

August 2, 1993

Rev. Paul Sinclair
Church On The High Road
Elim Church
334 High Road
Willesden, London
NW10 2EN, England

Dear Rev. Sinclair:

    I was very pleased to receive your telephone call in response to my July 21, 1993 letter. Thank you.

    On behalf of Clint Eastwood and personally, please accept our thanks as well for understanding our concerns regarding your use of Mr. Eastwood's likeness and slogans and for agreeing to remove them upon your return to England within the next several weeks. We do appreciate your understanding.

    I will continue to think through your comment regarding forgiveness and permission. It is a very funny line which I will use, but with attribution.

    Again, thank you for your response and your courtesy.

    Sincerely,

By

cc: Clint Eastwood

By chance I was off to America the very next week after receiving these letters so I put the 'Go ahead, make my Day' sign up, so when I arrived there I called Clint's attorney. He was a real nice guy and admitted they had all loved the posters, but regrettably had to prevent a precedent where just anyone could use Clint Eastwood's picture. In fun I pointed out, 'the problem is we think differently because you're a lawyer and I'm a minister. I believe it's easier to ask forgiveness than permission.' In the best American fashion a win-win situation was found, as I couldn't take it down until I got back to England and was taking it down then anyway, I was on my word I would and that would be my deadline.

However, mentioning all this to my local newspaper I had no idea of the furore that would follow. This was almost a disaster as the first news agency journalist had written a scathing article about Clint's attorneys. Fortunately when I called in later I discovered this and someone else changed it. The story then went national and international with TV and radio coverage!

One can only wonder how Clint would have played Jesus in a movie: 'Now listen, Legion, did I fast for six days or was it only five? I guess in all this excitement I clean forgot. Seeing as this is the Word of God – the most powerful handbook in the world and would blow your head clean off, you've got to ask yourself a question. Do I feel lucky? So go ahead, punk, make me pray!'

South Brent Observer

THURSDAY, SEPTEMBER 9, 1993   061-427 4404

SHOWDOWN WITH CLINT

Poster gets vicar in a fistful of trouble

Forgiven..by The Unforgiven

COME to CHURCH "Make my Day!"

Dirty Harry makes vicar's day!

COMING (TO THIS CHURCH) NEXT WEEK

THE FORGIVEN

GED

The local traffic wardens one day made front page of the *Willesden and Brent Chronicle*. One unlucky warden suffered 'the second brutal beating of his five-month career'. This poor soul was grabbed from behind by three thugs who pulled his crash helmet off and used it as a weapon against him, they 'knocked him to the ground where they kicked and punched him, before stroking ignited matches across his face'. On his first day in the job that same man was even bitten!

With double-yellow lines outside our church door it was inevitable someone would get caught at some point. On one occasion a newspaper photographer got a ticket while taking a picture of one of the signs and during this time I had a car and it actually got towed away! But no one deserved treatment, a beating, like that poor soul. Even in the face of violence our local traffic wardens kept their chin up and made a point of always commenting on our signs. It was time to cheer them up and let them join in on a gag.

A merry heart does good like medicine.
Proverbs 17:22

Being conscious of traffic wardens constant suffering the last thing I wanted to do was make things worse so I bounced the idea for this sign off one of the wardens first. Seeing the funny side, I had their blessing, just the ticket! A passing journalist spotted the sign and before we knew it we had made Page 3 of the *Sun*. Best of all, the son of one of our traffic wardens, Max, travelled all the way from Essex to visit us and despite the enormous distance became one of our most hard- working and respected members.

Thy wheel be done!

VICAR DECLARES WAR ON TRAFFIC WARDENS

Sun exclusive

Above: One of the signs by my Wayside Pulpit mentor the Rev. Brian Grist.

The church was growing and I had been ordained. Things were on the up. But news heard at an earlier church growth seminar continued to haunted me. We were shown an American statistic of an area where the census included the number of church-going Christians. Over twenty years in this area a supersize mega-church had grown up. This mega-church was a superb example of what a church *could* be with thousands in its auditorium, sports facilities, community programmes and so forth, but when they counted the number of church-going folk in the next census they discovered the number of church attendees in the area was still the same. The Christians had simply switched church! Doing what you do better than other churches will bring transfers and catering for needs missed by other churches will bring transfers as well, but it is hardly inspirational to think some day you will look back and think, 'Yes, I pinched the whole lot of them!'

There was no fear of me achieving that as I'd started with a tiny congregation in a near-derelict church down the street from three superb churches with better facilities, all bigger by hundreds and with great church clergy to boot, so our Wayside Pulpit was designed for folk who don't go to church. Most un-churched folk believe there is a God and some even know the Gospel, so our signs were targeted at them.

After some years I asked how many had come to our church as a result of seeing our signs. A full three quarters of the congregation put their hands up. Our Wayside Pulpit had passed the test; we had grown at no cost to the other churches on our street. Obviously this also reflected on just how good the other churches were, but for us it proved we were Soul Agents.

The Holy Spirit is the Spirit of Truth, but that does not mean he is predictable and boring. In one of our services my sermon was on God using and anointing our hands. At the end I asked everyone to hold out their hands and ask God to anoint them and use them. One very reliable member came forward, she was shaking and her hands were covered in oil. I asked her why on earth she had poured oil on her hands and she insisted she hadn't, it had just appeared. I was about to comment, but it dawned on me we didn't have any oil in the church and I could see there wasn't any where she had been sitting either. This seemed ridiculous, but I couldn't deny what I saw. 'Well you'd better lay hands on folk,' I said in a rather bewildered tone. So she did and each person she touched was thrown back with great force and really affected by this.

Visiting our congregation the following Sunday was a respected local girl in training for the mission field and this time the oil appeared on her as well. I asked anyone who was ill to go to those who had oil appearing on their hands for prayer. People came forward and as these two ladies touched them they were forcibly knocked backwards. With no one to catch them they crashed over chairs. It was untidy, but very real! Everyone prayed for was clearly affected and there was no doubt among us that God was doing these things.

**For the time will come when men will not put up with sound doctrine.
Instead, to suit their own desires,
they will gather around them a great number of teachers
to say what their itching ears want to hear.
2 Timothy 4:3**

The Holy Spirit can heal people and, undoubtedly, does do unusual things in services, but this is when he wants to do so and we have to accept the fact that sometimes he doesn't rather than try to make it up! There are times when God just wants you to build your faith, to think, to listen, to study, to do good deeds, to sacrifice, to serve others, to repent or to give. The only thing you might feel at such times is the desire for a cup of tea, but the Holy Spirit is not ours to command, he is our commander. Bookshops provide off-the-shelf spirituality techniques that provide a high, but only the Truth will make you free, so if you visit a service where God isn't doing anything dramatic it doesn't mean he is not there, it just means he wants to do something different.

MISSION IMPOSSIBLE ?
WITH GOD
ALL THINGS
ARE POSSIBLE.
EXPECT THE IMPOSSIBLE EVERY SUNDAY - 11:00AM

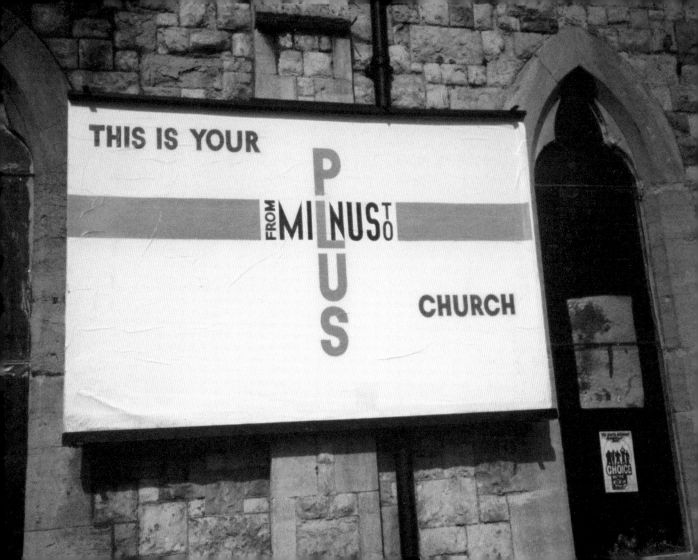

he writing was on the wall - our church was due to be sold by Brent Council. However, what the council did not bank on was Her Majesty the Queen, Defender of the Faith stepping in to help.

Bearing in mind that our nineteenth-century Congregational Chapel had been a derelict shell when we took it over and it was our congregation who had restored the place to a fully working church it did seem a bit unfair, and steep, that we were expected to pay for the increased value if we wanted to buy it! My predecessor Phyllis Preudhomme came out of retirement to stand with us as we took up this fight and she wrote to both Brent Council and the press for support. Oblivious to the mail-merge facility on my computer, I worked a straight 27 hour shift writing to each and every local councillor who could help. Letter after letter after letter, each individually targeted, many similar, but no two the same. We wrote to many people asking for their support, but all to no avail – it seemed we were up against highly motivated and able people on a mission to sell our church from underneath us.

So, one of our elders, James Hayes, and one member, Ian Paul Forbes, wrote to the Queen in her capacity as Defender of the Faith to she if she could offer us a hand. With remarkable speed and command, Her Majesty acted and a few days later my telephone rang. 'You spoke to The Queen!' the shocked and horrified voice of Brent's appointed property man squealed at me, '*The Queen!*'.

Brent Council had no choice but to drop their plans and let us buy the church instead. They had to take into account the 40 years work of our congregation, accept a significantly lower sum and then permit us to pay it off at an affordable rate interest free. God save the Queen!

Our church was now open Sundays and has been ever since.

I wanted to buy the bookmakers next door. Apart from the fact we desperately needed a place for our children and youth to go I knew that it used to belong to the church and this bothered me. Almost a century ago the church was condemned and sold off in two parts. Despite this the main church later re-opened as Neman's Billiards Hall, which was also famous for the sign outside. 'Neman's Billiards Hall, come inside and be a New Man,' it proclaimed. Infamously, the billiards hall witnessed a murder and eventually the church was condemned again.

What has been will be again, what has been done will be done again; there is nothing new under the sun.
Ecclesiastes 1:9-14

Meanwhile, the neighbouring house carried on as a shop until becoming a bookmaker, most famously a Playboy Bookmaker. With William Hill Bookmakers now occupying what were formally church premises I wanted those premises back! My first strategy was to walk in and ask for it, but that didn't work, so I wrote letters and made calls to the head office, again to no avail. To get their attention I placed the sign, opposite, outside. This certainly got the attention of the local punters but my picture of it with a letter met with defeat at William Hill's HQ. After some more attempts I received a polite, but 'final letter' saying no.

Before one Sunday church service began a man called Peter Obadan came in and saw me staring hopelessly at this 'final letter'. Peter is a big Nigerian man who first attended our church because of the 'Now Open Sundays!' telephone directory advert. I showed him the 'final letter' from William Hill. Obviously noting my look of defeat he asked if he could take it into the service. Although I was discouraged I guessed he was up to something, so said yes. Peter took this 'final letter' from William Hill Bookmakers into the service, stood at the front, held it up, explained what it was and then ripped it up with the words, 'In Jesus's name I have cancelled it!' Peter is now known as Reverend Obadan and presently works for the Nigerian government.

The earth is the Lord's and everything in it
Psalm 24:1

Any rejection or discouragement was blown away in an instant! The bookies was set aside for God's purpose – not gambling, it wasn't the written words of William Hill that mattered, it was God's written words! For years this place had been a bookmaker, but over a hundred years ago someone would have dedicated it to God. This final letter was cancelled and ripped up and the members agreed to fast and pray for one day each week and that night we took all the cooking oil we could find and splashed it over William Hill's walls and across the pavement in front to anoint the bookies. We had no money and no clue what to do next, but now we had faith.

I knew our Wayside Pulpit was a great tool, but it hadn't worked on its own so this time I would use my motorbike. Standing in my lock-up with a pen and paper I devised a plan. Writing down all the names and addresses on each tin of polish, oil, cleaning materials, the tyres and numerous other bike-related things, I began to write letters.

My plan was to do some fun stuff on my bike in the hope of gaining brand sponsorship and positive PR. It was vital I wasn't perceived as attacking William Hill because as the bible says, Love your neighbour, but equally I needed financial and press support if I was to succeed. Soon after I began my new task, I was asked to pose for a motorbike magazine and my local kids helped by treating the bike with my newly sponsored Mer polish, but they also polished the seat! At the photoshoot I decided to pull a stoppie – this is when you pull on the front brake so hard the back wheel flips into the air – and, unfortunately, I slid violently down the polished seat and into the tank at such an alarming speed that, as Bertie Simmonds the journalist put it, 'more than one lump came to his throat!'

This minor setback aside, many motorbike companies sent money, parts and products to help raise funds. Some lent their PR agencies, others their own staff and contacts. I only knew a few stunts so I started with a simple burnout. Revving it a bit high the church disappeared in smoke, but despite that the photo made a full page in *MotorCycle News* called 'Holy Smoke!' As I named sponsors on the bike Bridgestone sent tyres and a told me to 'Keep the Faith'. Someone locally targeted my £130 tyres with nails, so without Bridgestone I would never have made it. Six months after starting my questionable PR stunt-riding career to gain attention to our cause I was awarded *Bike Magazine*'s 'Man of the Year.' Modeling the *Shawshank Redemption* I sent copies of the press clippings to the William Hill directors with a letter explaining the need of that building for our church. I did not let up and added, 'I will not let you go until you bless me'. Again I would write, 'I will not let you go until you bless me'. In the end the Managing Director of the bookmakers, Mr John Brown, sent a truly 'final letter' with £100 cheque, enough to cover my previous postage and the words 'Bless you!'

THANKS TO *William* HILL

THIS CHURCH IS NOW
A SAFE BET!!

"SOME TRUST IN... HORSES.
BUT WE TRUST IN THE NAME OF THE LORD OUR GOD."
(PSALM 20:7)

THIS BOOKIES WAS BOUGHT
FOR THE CHURCH
BY TONY McGOVERN
HE THOUGHT IT WAS CHEAPER
TO BUY THE BUILDING
THAN TO KEEP USING IT
ON A WEEKLY BASIS

In the end, William Hill Bookmakers had agreed to relocate and sell us their property so we wound up being the only church in the UK regularly praying for a gambling business to find better premises, but when the time did come to move we didn't have the money required. Now, no one has a bigger heart for the Willesden community than Tony McGovern so I made an appointment to go see him. As a successful local businessman he is nobody's fool and wanted to test my sincerity to the cause and congregation, so he'd secretly planned a test for me. Tony offered to 'take the problem off my hands' in such a way it would leave the congregation so much better off we'd actually make a profit. The goal, I told him, was not to make a profit so I politely refused. So, he then made an even better offer, but I wasn't going to compromise after so many years of faithful service even if his final 'offer' would let me walk away with a large sum in my pocket and 'No one will know.' Tony winked. 'God would!' I countered. A grin appeared as he knew I wouldn't budge on his offer – then he laughed out loud, 'There's been a few people who've sat in that chair and given a different answer to you!' Tony said. It had all been a test and everyone in the building knew about it except me. He was making sure he was backing the right horse. Joyfully he shouted that I 'couldn't be bought' and 'get the cheque book!'

Mr. McGovern went on to supply double glazing for the entire church and supported us when a storm blew off the bookies roof, but I then had my road accident. Tony's long-term desire was to see a lunch club for the elderly commence, but this I would have to pass on to my successors. I introduced Tony to the bishop and our board sent a promise of every penny back if the lunch club was not finished after my leaving. He hadn't asked for this but I was taking no chances! After all, I'd no idea who would follow me and although I'd just bought a bookies, I'm certainly not a gambler!

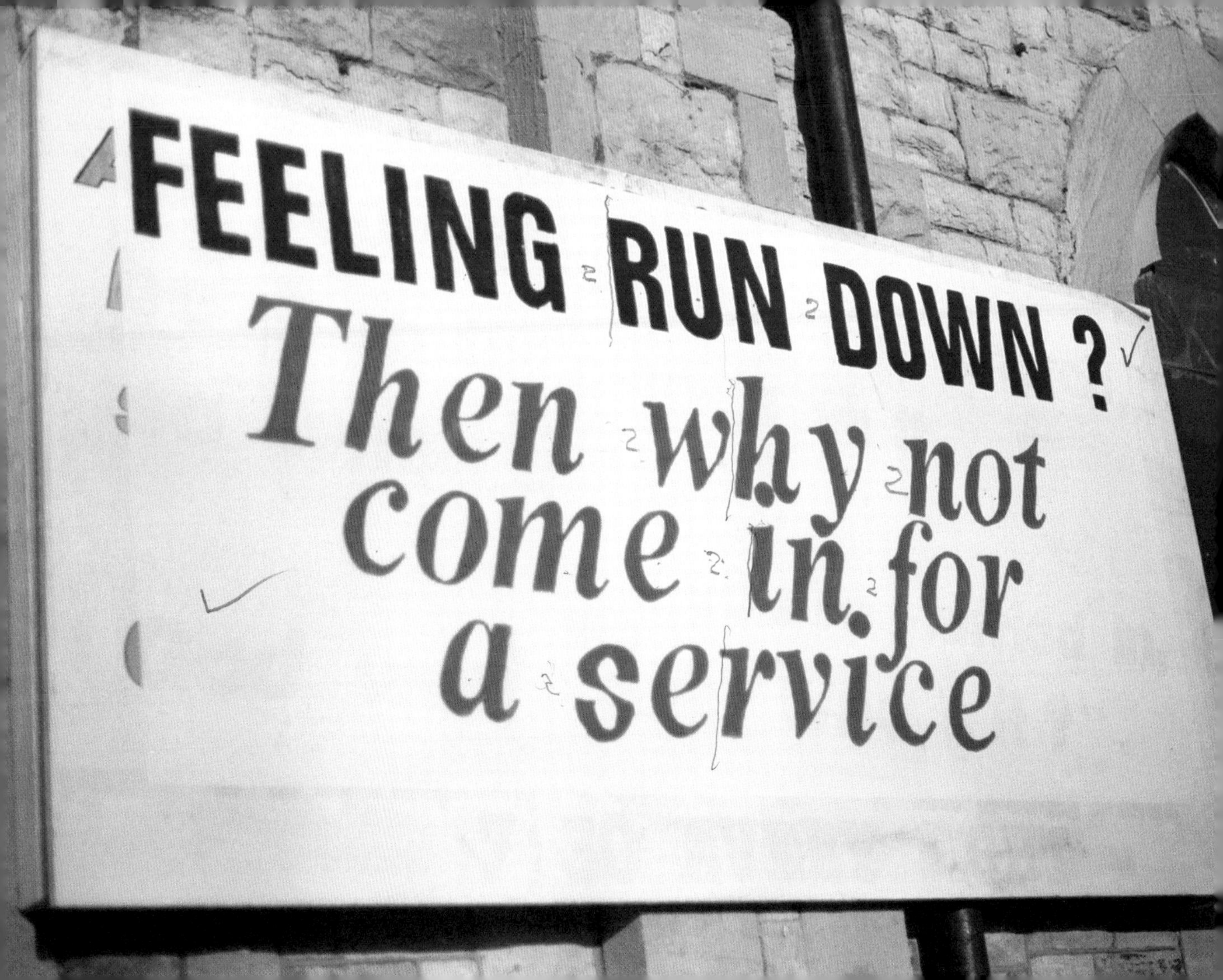
FEELING RUN DOWN ?
Then why not
come in for
a service

oon after we bought the bookmakers next door its roof was blown off in a storm. Most people would have their bet on the church roof blowing off so who says gamblers never win? All three floors were trashed and flooded and during a service my beloved motorbike was stolen. The thieves waited until we were singing so that we wouldn't hear the alarm! My trainee assistant was hospitalised, my mother had cancer operations and even the church computer died. As icing on the cake we were robbed and I wound up working as a motorcycle courier again to make ends meet. As if that wasn't enough my next bike was destroyed in a crash. My fiancée, now wife, Marian suffered a fracture, internal bashes and I was off in metalwork for months. With neither health nor income we cancelled our wedding, although churches, friends and colleagues ensured I kept my home and William Hill bookmakers gave me a laptop.

Even youths grow tired and weary, and young men stumble and fall;
but they that wait upon the LORD shall renew their strength;
they shall mount up with wings as eagles;
they shall run, and not be weary; they shall walk and not faint.
Isaiah 40:30-31

Professional people and those who face life's challenges wear down, dry up and burn out. No one can survive battles, knocks and bashes forever. Determination and mind over matter can even make things worse, so something else is needed. This is where religion can't cut it, but knowing God can. Knowing the Lord and experiencing His anointing is not just for the Goody Two Shoes, but for the worn down and weary.

As a growing multi-racial congregation we inevitably became a multi-cultural and multi-lingual church too so we launched Romanian and French-speaking African services as well. Pastor Tito is a man who believes in God and I can remember clearly him visiting one of our English-speaking members who had cancer. This chap had lost his hair and been really suffering with the treatment, to look at him hardly built faith, but Pastor Tito brought the faith with him! Soon this man was free and remained free.

Meanwhile, our Romanian membership rapidly overtook the rest of us though strangely enough I don't recall any of our ladies ever complaining about having to cope with anywhere between 80 and 200 very macho men so far from home! One Sunday we were truly shocked to hear four lettered swear words hurled at us by the preacher. Despite our clear shock he continued to repeat these all the more forcefully. Realising what was happening one translator explained that the Romanian phrase for 'do it' sounds identical to one four lettered swear word and they also have a descriptive single word for 'turning a table as you lift it' that sounds like another swear word. Oblivious to this, this good and sincere man had been passionately preaching on 'Do it, turn your life around.' After the translator's explanation he was desperately embarrassed. The Romanians were disciplined and serious men, powerful singers and extremely hard working, so much so Dave O'Keefe Building Suppliers stayed open late to supply them as they transformed our dilapidated building. Walking with God often means walking with people from different backgrounds, cultures and view points, which is difficult, but if you keep within The Maker's guidelines you do get the lifetime guarantee.

For me, personally, having a multi-racial, and multi-cultural, congregation meant becoming involved with the Rockers, motorcyclists and even a few hardcore bikers from the local area. My friend Simon Fletcher is such an example. A tough biker – he calls himself Satan – his ambition is to give the original Satan a good kicking if he was ever to see him! As a former cage fighter, and military man, I reckon Simon could, but what I can't get him to grasp is that there is no need, because Jesus has already done it!

ALMOST 2000 YEARS OLD
AND STILL UNDER
THE MAKER'S GUARANTEE

Most pastors go through phases where they lie awake at night pre-occupied with how many sheep attend their services and, just to compound this, most folk go off on holiday the week the Bishop is invited. Fortunately I was blessed with a huge Bishop called Phil Weaver who was convinced I only invited him and his wife to fill the front row.

Our Romanian membership had grown so large they really needed their own church and I did the paperwork to get them a pastor from Timisoara, but as the clock ticked to his arrival the stress of giving away over two thirds of our congregation really got to me. Although the launch of London's first Romanian Pentecostal Church would be a success I knew the resulting drop in our number would be perceived as failure.

I went for a walk round London with Andy McIlree, a senior Scottish minister. As we talked I was embarrassed to recognise so much pride, denial and stress in myself, but the irony of my pride in counting these sheep was that it was the Romanians that had built the Romanian congregation, not me and God was calling these hard working men 'through' our church, not 'to' our church. They had transformed the facilities and we had given them a launch pad, but it was time to send them forth to do what they then did, become a very successful church.

May the grace of the Lord Jesus Christ, and the love of God, and the fellowship of the Holy Spirit be with you all.
2 Corinthians 13:14

Andy Mac, as folk know him, reminded me to fellowship with the Holy Spirit by simply talking to him so later I began to do just that, got my peace back and finally stopped losing sleep!

ave O'Keefe Timber Suppliers was based a few yards from our church and if ever there was a young man who stood out it was Dave O'Keefe Junior. Built like a door, you wouldn't want to fall out with him, but equally he was honest, hard-working, discerning and someone who had a great ability to both listen and empathise. People tend to forget that Jesus was like that. He was no wimp. Jesus was amongst the ranks of real working men such as joiners and sheet iron workers. He didn't just work Sundays either. Jesus was a working man and the Apostle Paul likewise. They had demanding jobs, they had to get up early and when Jesus talked about minding his father's business he knew exactly what real business meant.

> ### Do you see a man skilled in his work?
> ### He will serve before kings;
> ### he will not serve before obscure men.
> ### Proverbs 22:29

Being a Christian isn't just going to church on Sunday to find God, it is walking with God in your workplace and living a life that God can be associated with and complement. There is nothing weak or whimsical about joining God, in truth it can be very difficult and tempting to give up, but real men don't mind hard work and know the rewards of it too. There is of course one other advantage of working for God – the pension benefits are out of this world.

ALL SERVICES ARE
DIFFERENT, WE LEAVE
THE REPEATS TO TV
WITH THANKS TO 'OFFICIAL' STATIONERS HIGH RD.

I'm not supposed to admit this, but trying to find a fresh angle on Christmas gets wearisome year after year. You are obliged to avoid repeats and find some astonishing new angle on the one story everyone knows inside out. All this on some pagan god's birthday!

At Christmas TV bosses fare no better than us with repeat after repeat after repeat. Some television executives actually take this a step further and determine to not only show the old repeats, but create new ones. Through many different approaches, such as news, documentary, soap, comedy and film, brand-new repeats are created where preachers are repeatedly portrayed as dull, dodgy, corrupt or camp. Rather than find the truth or create a new angle the viewing public is repeatedly presented with a well-worn doctrine on homosexuality, evolution, marriage, sex, abortion, death and ethics. Seeing themselves as modern-day cardinals these particular bosses decide what their preachers, sorry presenters and producers, should continuously repeat. Not only are we continually told what to believe about evolution, but even how we should perceive those who don't believe in it. Creationists are repeatedly portrayed as ignorant extremists while evolutionists are presented as scientifically sound intellectuals. All this from people who portray church as dull and repetitive!

Professing themselves to be wise, they became fools.
Romans 1:22

Most people are happy to see their local clergy trying to help folk in their communities, particularly in places where there is obvious need. Local Willesden folk, with no church affiliation whatsoever, helped us with our building requirements, practical needs and sometimes even with hard earned cash when we really needed it. Televised atheists – those people in the media who are very vocal in the opinions about God – however, are often scathing and quick to put down religion and our efforts and, seemingly, take great pride in explaining how we ministers are wasting our time and even accuse us of being a danger to the communities we serve, even though we dedicate our time helping a great deal of people in the community.

Some Atheists say Christians are foolish to believe that God created the heavens and the earth. They tell us that there simply cannot be no God and that in the beginning was nothing and that nothing came together with nothing to cause an explosion called the Big Bang. This explosion sent out particles from nothing to create the well ordered and amazing universe, not to mention the beauty of life, as we know it. If there was an explosion, as they claim, who lit the fuse? And where did the particles that were dispelled all over the universe come from as well?

What is more foolish? To believe God can create everything *for a purpose* or believe that nothing can explode something out of nothing?

L eonard Albert talks too fast to be a speaker and too slow to be a preacher, so he calls himself 'The Spreacher.' Leonard once told me his mum was a Jehovah's Witness and his dad an atheist so when he was a little boy he used to go round knocking on doors for no reason whatsoever!

After this sign went up two Jewish people wrote letters of appreciation, a few locals introduced themselves as Jewish fans of our signs and one lady even sent a cheque. Us Scots and the Jews suffer the same unfair reputation when it comes to writing cheques, so much so a South American preacher once asked me if it was true Scotsmen only become Christians because the Gospel is free. What he failed to grasp was that if money was the motivating factor then the religion that is cheapest at Christmas would be the one to go for.

In the few short miles around our church we went through a spate of shootings and vicious muggings with one poor soul carried off from right outside the door, I never found out if he lived or died. Throughout that dark period it was encouraging to know our good humour helped the neighbours keep smiling. During such times it is easy to forget that most folk are discouraged and embarrassed when their neighbourhood is reflected in a bad light.

A cheerful heart is good medicine, but a crushed spirit dries up the bones. Proverbs 17:22

In twelve years I can only ever remember one critic of our Wayside Pulpit in the whole of Brent – an atheist! When we posted our 'International Atheist Day – April 1st' sign, he was so unhappy he even reported me to Willesden Green Police station. God bless him, I was so delighted with his reaction I kept it up another month!

As well as this forbidden fruit caption you will find another Adam and Eve sign in this book, but there are two more: 'It wasn't the apple in the tree that caused the problem, it was the pear on the ground' and 'Eve was so jealous of Adam she used to count his ribs each night when he came home.'

Forbidden fruit is often related to sex outside of marriage and some unfortunates do find themselves forbidden to get any of that kind of fruit even within marriage, but we won't go there right now. Sex beyond God's parameters and lack of sex within them does cause harm, but there are other poisonous fruits that do considerable damage as well.

Get rid of all bitterness, rage and anger, brawling and slander, along with every form of malice.
Ephesians 4:31

When my dad was in the navy they once fired a torpedo at a huge iceberg. It slid up, did a pirouette at the top and came straight back at them, 'talk about getting your own back,' he exclaimed. Malice is like that, it eats away at you until you finally let loose your best shot, only to watch it sliding straight back at you.

Offering forgiveness can make things even more frustrating. If you offer forgiveness or an apology only to have it slapped back in your face it is natural to simmer and boil. Everyone has an outburst from time to time, even Jesus did that when he entered the temple, but long-standing bitterness, simmering rage and all-consuming anger is a fruit that eats you.

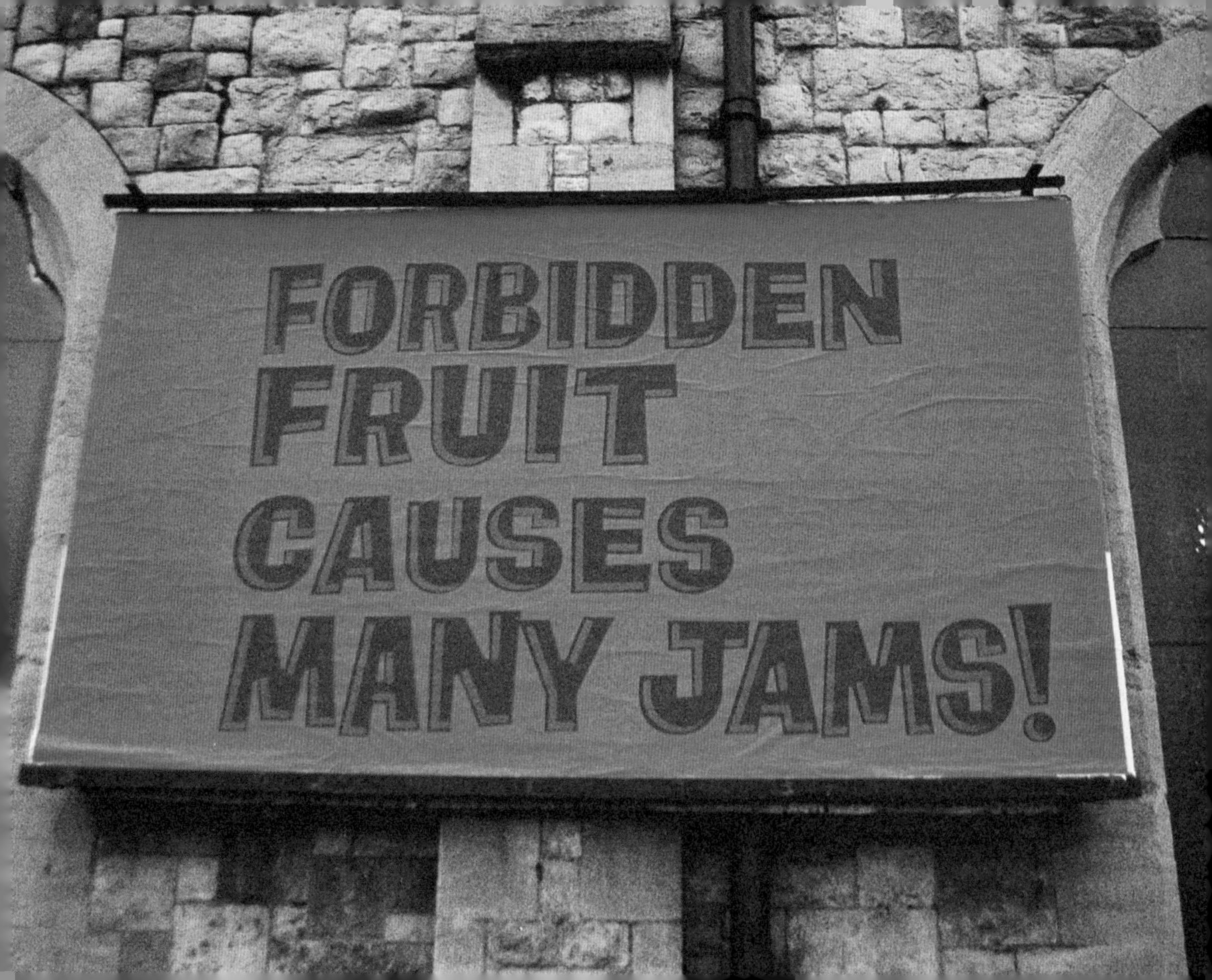
FORBIDDEN
FRUIT
CAUSES
MANY JAMS!

A member of a well-known biker club invited me to attend an important event, but accidently gave the wrong date. Complete with clerical shirt I rode the full 120 miles to find only five bikes outside. A large man with a white beard answered the door and as he pointed out the meeting was the day before he saw my face fall. 'It's the thought that counts' he assured me with the warmest possible handshake. Another 120 miles later I made it home. Despite their fearsome reputation the biker who invited me gave the most heartfelt apology possible.

Paradoxically, I challenged a Christian whose career appears to be on the slide to apologise to people he had let down. Listening to his well-rehearsed response it was evident I wasn't the first to advise him, 'You can't unscramble eggs,' he explained in sermon mode. I agreed, but the person who scrambled them should still apologise. When I quoted facts the shell of respectability cracked quicker than those eggs and an annoyed retort was fired, 'Have you never made mistakes?' Of course, I could write a book on my mistakes, 'well, there you are' and he bolted off.

Many are put off church by Christians who are not perfect and even more when they know really good folk who don't go, but avoidance itself is a mistake because the whole point in church is to recognise you are a flawed individual saved by Grace. The other thing it is natural to forget is that those people will give an account to God some day, so whether they give an account to you or not is irrelevant!

For all have sinned, and come short of the glory of God.
Romans 3:23

illesden Green Library has the best live bands, best food and runs all sorts of creative events. It even has books! Their progressive head David Jones sponsored this poster. Church should be creative too. The bible kicks off with, 'In the beginning God created...' so we sought creative ways to present the Gospel. A group of girls called Soul to Soul ran a fashion show complete with catwalk and models and we invited great musical groups. The question hanging over creativity is just how far do you go? I was keen to perch a huge vulture on the roof with the caption, 'Some people are like vultures, they only come to church when someone dies!' But my fear of a funeral taking place made me cancel it. As our congregation were a lively bunch who loved to belt out hymns I planned an adaptation of the famous Alien movie poster caption from, 'In space, no one can hear you scream' to 'In a Pentecostal Church no one can hear you scream'. I still laugh at that one, but I figured the elders might not! The closest poster to the Alien movie I did go for was a spoof of the popular X-Files 'The truth is out there' series of the time. Ours said, 'The truth is in here'.

My one Wayside Reject Deluxe was to convince another pastor nearby to join me in a spoof poster war. I'd put up, 'we are the best church in Willesden' to which they would then retort, 'we are the biggest church in Willesden,' then I'd follow through with, 'We may be half the size, but we are twice as righteous!' As I excitedly ran my idea past the other reverend I realised he was looking at me in abject horror, so I shut up.

IF YOU WANT
TO READ
66 GOOD BOOKS
BUY A BIBLE

WILLESDEN GREEN

LIBRARY

ANY MORE THAN THAT, GO TO WILLESDEN GREEN LIBRARY at Nº 95

NINE out of **TEN CATS**... *agree that their owners need* **SALVATION!**

The message of the Gospel must be preached to every tribe, so being part of the motorcycling tribe I held a televised Biker's Service at the Burton upon Trent Elim Pentecostal Church. We utilised the wheelchair ramp and cleared the chairs so that the bikes could be ridden inside. Officially this was to host a custom show before the service, unofficially it was to make sure anyone not wanting to hear the gospel could not get on their bike.

Before the service started I noticed a West Indian man who was upset. He had wanted to bring his bike but his wife wouldn't let him. When asked what sort of bike it was, he said an exercise bike! This Biker's Service was featured in Robbie Coltrane's *B-Road Britain* so let me take you to an even greater destination in A-Road Rome...

For the wages of sin is death,
but the gift of God is eternal life in Christ Jesus our Lord.
Romans 6:23

But God demonstrates his own love for us in this:
While we were still sinners, Christ died for us.
Romans 5:8

That if you confess with your mouth, "Jesus is Lord,"
and believe in your heart that God raised him from the dead, you will be saved.
Romans 10:9

The A-Road to God is not a process of perfectionism; although once you get there it does involve the annoying process of realising you really did need to know God, because if you can still make a pig's ear of life with him what possible chance did you ever have without him? The A-Road to God is realising you'll never make the grade with God and it is downright foolishness to even try to win him over. No matter what you do it will never be enough and this is why you need the Gospel. The Gospel is the Good News and the Good News is that in confessing Jesus is Lord and repenting you can be free of your sin to reach the ultimate destination.

While in Willesden I was made an area leader responsible for nearly a dozen churches, but since then my name has plummeted through the Denominational Year Book lists from senior minister, to minister, to non-voting minister and ultimately to such a depth they have just about run out of Year Book lists! This is the clergy equivalent of my being moved from Class 2B at Penilee Secondary School to Class 3K the following year. Things are looking up though as the results of my sidecar-hearse service has resulted in the decision to create a new list for those who 'work more independently of our denominational structures and vision.' Recognition at last, onwards and upwards!

Success should be encouraged, but success without God is delusion and therefore no success at all. One successful millionaire became a Christian and people sneered at him, 'Why do you need God, what does it matter what happens when you are dead?' 'Well,' he replied, 'it matters because you'll be dead a lot longer than you'll be alive!' One day your money, your status and all you own will be left behind.

What does it profit a man if he gains the whole world, but loses his soul?
Mark 8:36

When we die and stand before God our assets, finance, status and even my Penilee School Report Card will all be left behind so without a relationship with God nothing we have now will be worth anything at all.

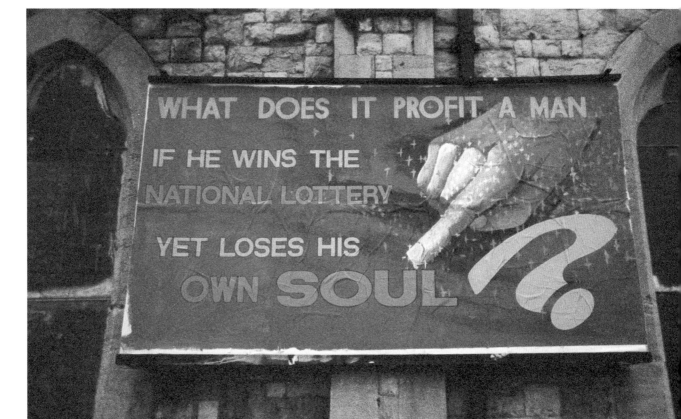

Think about GOD...

| God did'nt call them TEN SUGGESTIONS | Did it ever occur to you that Nothing occurs to GOD | God so loved the World that He did'nt send a committee |

When it was time to move I wrote my resignation on the same day as Michael Portillo wrote his. Watching the media furore I lost sight of reality and began to think that I too would be heralded as a hero in our little denomination. Overall the press was kind to Michael Portillo and I imagined a similar immediate accolade to be faxed across immediately, 'Well done Paul, fantastic job, couldn't have done it better myself.' The next day I kept close to the fax.

Seven months and two weeks later I received a written reply. I guess I wasn't quite up there with Michael Portillo in anyone else's imagination after all. It was a full nine years later before the national newspapers contacted me, then finally Portico Books, and here you are.

The fear of the Lord teaches a man wisdom, and humility comes before honour.
Proverbs 15:33

The good news is that you do not need to wait ten years before you appear in a book. Not only that, you can appear in a more expensive book that will last a lot longer too. It's called the Lamb's Book of Life. That is where the names of those who know the Lord are recorded. Although you may not be aware of it there are a few other books you are already in, one being the book of your life with warts and all presented. One day that will be opened and you will be judged according to every bad deed and sin listed within it. But the Good News is that if you get yourself entered in the Lamb's Book of Life it over rules the others, will never go out of print and is permanently bound.

The Journeys of Paul: A Final Word

I've two-finger-typed as fast as I can to hopefully bring you laughter, entertain and make you think, but what should you do now? I once climbed to the top-level diving board of a championship swimming pool. I knew I'd be safe if I jumped because buoyancy would push me back up and although I was a good diver I didn't even need to dive head first, I could simply jump, but despite my knowledge fear came over me as I faced this leap of faith, and I climbed back down. Just as I knew it was safe to jump into the water, you now know that to jump into a walk with God is an adventure and that if you repent and confess him as Lord you will be saved, but as with any jump of faith you fear the consequences. I failed to make that jump of faith off the diving board, but you needn't have faith as weak as mine. Take the consequences seriously, but don't fail to take the jump!

Jesus Christ died at a young age so that we could live forever. On this earth we may not all live to be 95 but with Jesus as Lord of your life that is nothing to how long you will live in eternity. This is the message of this book and our Wayside Pulpit, that I am not ashamed of the Gospel of Christ, for it is the power of God that brings salvation to everyone who believes. Romans 1:16.

Above right: Paul, with wife Marian, Measham, 2010

Acknowledgements

Thousands of people were involved in our story and we are grateful for them all. To avoid offending anyone I only list those directly involved in the writing of this book.

Robert Pollock (Introduction)
Mary Pryce-Williams (Front Cover)
George Miller (Foreword)
Charles Ankrr Hammond (Last services until the M1)
Steve Vanzant (Sermons delivered hot)
Raquel Sims (Don't think that God)
Eileen Christie (The bible should be trusted)
Richard Essandoh (Black is also available)
Gordon Sinclair (Forbidden fruit)
Tim Emmett (God is perfect)

Photography on page 32 © Theresa Wassif. All photography taken by the author unless marked otherwise.
Photography not taken by the author has been used with permission.

For the sake of protecting his career I should point out Rev. Gordon Neale, my Bishop, had no part in this book whatsoever.

The following people could not help me directly as they are no longer with us, but as they were very much on my mind while writing they deserve special mention:
Charlotte Moir Baxter Pollock
Fred the neighbour
John Bagnall
Leah Vanzant
Mrs Cox
Mrs Amory
Ray Pryce-Williams

Timmy Dillon
Rev John Barr
Rev Wynne Lewis

Many thanks to the good people at the publishers, in particularly, Katie Cowan, Zoe Anspach, Richard Cheshire and Malcolm Croft.

Special thanks to Zelda Croft.

To Mr Brown who has now retired from William Hill bookmakers – Bless you!

As a special treat for reading this far I'll let you in on a little secret. Prior to my arrival at the church, when the original lease was already drawn up, Brent council had put certain, legal, size restrictions on the signs that were permitted outside on the church wall. I think you will find our Wayside Pulpit exceeded them somewhat, by nearly double! I carried this dark secret for twelve years convinced there would one day be a knock on my door by some council authority – or worse, Police! – and, as I was led away for breaking the law, I would watch our famous sign be torn down! It never happened though despite all the interest we had in the signs over the years!

Published in the United Kingdom in 2010 by
Portico Books
10 Southcombe Street
London
W14 0RA

An imprint of Anova Books Company Ltd

ISBN 9781906032838

A CIP catalogue record for this book is available from the British Library.

10 9 8 7 6 5 4 3 2 1

Printed and bound in China by Imago

This book can be ordered direct from the publisher at
www.anovabooks.com

To learn more about Paul, please visit www.fasterpastor.com and
www.motorcyclefunerals.com